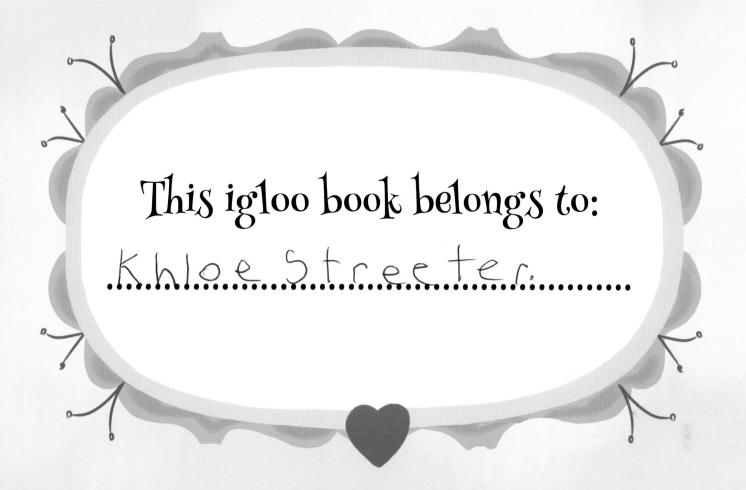

This igloo book belongs to:

K.hlo.e. Streeter..........

igloobooks

Published in 2017
by Igloo Books Ltd
Cottage Farm
Sywell
NN6 0BJ
www.igloobooks.com

REX001 0517
2 4 6 8 10 9 7 5 3
ISBN 978-1-78343-825-9

Written by Sienna Williams
Illustrated by Natalie Smillie

Printed and manufactured in China

Even Fairies Need Glasses

igloobooks

Cassie was a fairy who was quite misunderstood.
The problem was her eyesight, which wasn't very good.

It made her **very clumsy** and no matter how hard she tried, the magic spells she cast seemed to cause trouble far and wide.

Cassie needed to wear glasses, but the thought filled her with **dread**.

"I'm sure I will be teased," she thought, "with **those things** on my head."

On her first day of Fairy School, Cassie felt **really scared.**
"What if it all goes wrong?" she thought.

"I'm really not prepared!"

There were
bursts, sparks, and flashes,
then the teacher cried out, "STOP!"

"Cassie!" cried her fairy friends.
"You've messed up EVERY spell!"
She didn't want to tell them
that she couldn't see
too well.

The next time Cassie tried, she was desperate not to fail. She meant to make a rainbow...

... but instead, she made it hail.

She cast **frogs** instead of puppies.

Her **potions** all turned green.

The teacher thought her magic was the **worst** she'd ever seen.

Then it was time for flying class.
"Get ready!" the teacher cried.

"Grab a pinch of fairy dust and spread your wings out wide!"

Cassie hoped and wished that...

...just this once she might succeed...

... but she fell SPLASH into a puddle...

... and felt very sad indeed.

Poor Cassie flew away. She gave a **sob** and then a **howl**.
"Oh dear, why are you crying?" asked a funny-looking owl.

Cassie sniffed and said...

... "Without glasses, I can't see!"

"I can help," said Owl. "Why don't you follow me?"

Owl showed her **lots** of glasses,
everything from **big** to small.

Round glasses... ... square glasses...

... Cassie tried them all!

Suddenly, she saw some that were
all she'd ever dreamed.

They were twinkly
and sparkly.

They glinted and
they gleamed.

Cassie tried them on and straight away began to stare.

After seeing her reflection...

... she jumped up in the air!

"I can see!" cried Cassie. "These new glasses are just right".
So, she hurried back to school, almost bursting with delight.

From then on, Cassie's magic went **exactly** as she planned.

She had the **perfect** glasses...

... and the best spells in the land.

"Do that one again!" the whole class would start to cry, as Cassie swished her wand and **pretty butterflies** flew by.

By the end of term, Cassie was top of all her classes.
She could hardly believe it was all thanks to her new glasses.

"I'm **so happy**," said Cassie. "Whoever would have guessed that wearing my new spectacles would make my spells **the best!**"